New

J. Adams

ISBN-13: 978-0615651514
ISBN-10: 0615651518

Orlando, Florida

Today is going to be a great day to die.

I am a complete mess and I know it. I also know what you see when you look at me. As sure as I'm standing here, I know.

You see a broken down human being, who, at the moment, is more being than human. Worn, torn and bedraggled. Lame, not of body, but of heart and spirit. Frozen in time and place, longing to pick up the pieces of my life but not knowing how.

Someone nudges me and I move forward, taking the offered bowl from a smiling volunteer in the soup kitchen line. Finding an empty seat, I sit down, avoiding eye contact with the others at the table. I am acquainted with them, but I find no need to speak, and neither do they. We've shared the same address–the city park lawn–for the past year. Our stories have been shared countless times, and the lines etched into our weary faces tell those stories.

Richard, the guy to the right of me, owned an accounting firm that plunged along with the economy. He went bankrupt and lost everything, including his girlfriend and his many so-called friends. Amy, to the left, is a seventeen-year-old runaway who had been kicked out by her drug addict parents. And sitting directly in front of me is Mark. His gambling addiction robbed him of his once comfortable lifestyle.

Demons. We all face them every day that we are on the streets, and we strive to make sure our stories are not forgotten. Like we are.

My story, however, is the most painful.

A year ago I was a successful writer for a national magazine. I was a wife, a mother, a friend. My lifestyle was a comfortable one and I had everything I needed and more.

One afternoon changed everything.

✽✽✽

Coming home to an empty house is surprising, but that feeling immediately turns to shock as I enter my two-month-old baby girl's room to find her crib gone and the dresser drawers empty. Running to my room, a painful wail escapes me as I pull out empty drawers that had just this morning held my husband's clothes. Shaking my head in momentary denial, I try to make sense of it all. Then my frozen feet move. Just as I pick up the phone to call the police, the doorbell rings, making the call unnecessary.

I am told by the solemn officer that my husband has been in an accident. Jack, my little Heather and the woman with them all died. I have suspected Jack of cheating for a while now, but to take my baby . . .

Five long and emotional days later I am informed by the bank that because of missed payments (a complete shock and a mystery to me) my home is no longer mine and I need to vacate. Moving through a haze, I fill a backpack. Taking the five thousand dollars I have been secretly saving from its hiding place at the bottom of the cedar chest at the foot of our bed, I stuff it into my pocket and walk away.

After a three-month binge of drugs and alcohol, the money dwindles to nothing and the streets become my home.

***

Though no longer a drug and alcohol user, my life choices up to this point are clearly written all over my countenance and I am no longer able to see the real me. I have forgotten who I am. I am sick of heart and tired in spirit, and I have no desire to remain among the living, if you can call barely existing living.

I am insignificant, making no difference in the world, having no purpose, and no sense of worth. So I see no point in remaining among the living.

"I'm done," I whisper as I step from the curb into the path of an oncoming black SUV. *I am so done.*

***

Chance

Anticipating what the woman is attempting to do, Chance Hunter slams on his brakes, stopping within an inch of her slender form. Jumping out of the car, he runs to her. He briefly meets her intense gaze before catching her in his arms as her eyes slip shut and she passes out. Walking around to the passenger side, he gently places her in the seat, and then gets in and drives off.

Chance glances over at the woman every few seconds. Even with its gaunt appearance, he has never seen a more beautiful face. For weeks now, he has watched the woman from afar, wanting to help her but not knowing how.

And with each passing day, the guilt he has harbored is magnified. It had been his ex wife, Barbara, in the truck with the woman's husband. And though he had been saddened by her death, his loss was nothing compared to the woman's. Her husband had been unfaithful, true, but he took something from her that was both precious and priceless, something that can never be replaced.

A week after the accident, Chance stopped by to see her and offer his condolences, stunned to find she had left, evicted from her home after losing her child. Indeed, she'd lost everything.

Chance knows what it is like to lose so much. It has

been years, but it still makes him angry to think about what his ex wife had done. Barbara failed to inform him before they were married that she had undergone a hysterectomy months before the wedding because she didn't want children, concerned that pregnancy would 'mess up' her body. It had been one of the most selfish things Chance had ever seen someone do. Upon discovering this, he'd quickly filed for a divorce, losing a chunk of his accounting firm in the process, as well as his home. Selling the rest of his shares, he invested his money and started over.

Over the past year, he never stopped thinking about the woman in the seat next to him. He had longed to know what happened to her. He'd never met her, but he recognized her from a faded photograph found crumpled in the glove compartment of her husband's truck.

Then, last month on the way home, he had driven through the homeless section of Orlando and spotted her sitting on a bench in front of the shelter. He had desperately wanted to go to her, but he didn't want to frighten her away. So every day he has watched her from a parking lot down the street. This morning he'd finally decided to go to her, not knowing how timely his decision would be.

Pressing a gentle hand against the woman's cheek, he marvels at the intensity of his feelings. In a matter of weeks, he has fallen in love with this beautiful lost soul. Never has anything like this ever happened to him, not even with his ex wife. And now that the woman he adores is in his car close to him, he allows himself for the first time ever, to speak her name.

"Cosset."

❃❃❃

I slowly open my eyes, focusing my vision on the familiar steps leading up to the police station. The luxurious aroma of leather and cinnamon and apple fills me with warmth. I turn. The face of the man in the driver's seat is familiar and his kind hazel eye calm me, when reasonably, I should be freaking out right now.

"I have seen you before."

"We have never met."

I'm taken aback by the gentle cadence of his rich voice. "I have seen you driving by the shelter." Pulling my gaze from his, my eyes return to the station steps, and then the entrance. "Why did you bring me here?"

"I wanted to make sure when you awakened in a strange man's car, you would know there is no danger from me."

Well, considering what I was attempting to do, fear is the last thing I feel. "Why did you pick me up?"

"I want to help you."

I shoot him a skeptical look. "But you don't even know me."

He pauses. "I do . . . in a way. The woman in the truck with you late husband . . . she was my ex wife."

His shocking comment reopens painful wounds that have never healed. Leaning away from him, I open my mouth to speak, but he interrupts. "Cosset, listen to me," he continues, and I am startled to hear my real name spoken after a year of going by another. "We were divorced for a year when the accident happened. I came by your house that week to see you and tell you how sorry I was, but you were gone. You just disappeared."

Resting my head against the passenger door window, I close my eyes, releasing a deep sigh. "There was nothing left to keep me there. I lost everything." Blinking the tears back, I swallow hard against the rising emotion.

He takes my hand, giving it a comforting squeeze. "I know this is late, but I am so sorry."

I nod. There really isn't anything to say.

"Will you allow me to help you?"

"Help me how?" To say I am wary is putting it mildly." No one ever gives anything without expecting something in return.

As if he can read my mind, he again squeezes my hand, and strangely, I have no desire to pull it away. "I am offering you a job and a place to live. I only ask for your friendship, and maybe one day, your trust."

"That's a lot to ask," I whisper, meeting his beautiful gaze.

"I know." His voice is soft. "Can we try?"

This is without a doubt one of the hardest things I have been asked to do in a long time. This man is a stranger to me, yet he warmly offers me a second chance at life. How can I say no?

"What kind of job?" I finally ask.

"Well, how are your computer skills?"

11

I finally allow myself to smile. "They are pretty mad."

✻✻✻

"Tell me about your family," Chance says as we head to his place.

"Nothing much to tell, really. My younger brother and I were raised by a single mom. Mama died ten years ago on my eighteenth birthday. Cancer took her. Three years later while riding his bike on the way home from school, my brother was hit by a drunk driver. He died later that night. He was only seventeen."

"I'm sorry you have lost so many people close to you."

"It was a long time ago."

"What about your father?"

I'm surprised how quickly the memories come back. "I never knew my biological father, but my step-father, the man who really was a father to me, walked out of our lives when I was younger, and I haven't seen him since."

During a brief lapse in conversation, I allow my mind to drift back to the day my mother became a single parent once again.

My stepfather came home early from work. He usually put in so much overtime, it was rare to see him before eight o'clock at night. Mama was so happy to see him, she immediately went to him and wrapped her arms around his waist.

"Hi, baby. This is a big surprise! I'm so happy to see you!"

Standing in the kitchen doorway, I smiled as I watched them. The love Mama felt for Dave was clearly written on her face. From the day Mama met him, Dave held her heart in the palm of his hand. I had been eight and Nate four when they married, and Dave became our father. I grew to love him very much.

I watched the joyful look on Mama's face slowly disappear as Dave pushed her away and proceeded to tell her he didn't love her anymore, that there was another woman.

The abrupt silence in the room caused me to hold my breath, wondering what would happen next. I had noticed that Dave had been spending more and more time away from home. Mama always made excuses for him and reminded me of how hard he worked for us. But at that moment, I could see that something wasn't right.

"Is she the perfect blond-haired, blue-eyed girl your family always wanted you to marry?" Mama asked.

Dave turned to her, his expression surprisingly sad. "It's more complicated than that."

Those were the only other words spoken between them. He headed to their room to pack, leaving Mama rooted to the same spot, completely stunned.

"It's happening again," she softly murmured.

Mama held her head high until Dave was all packed and had left the house. Crying, I immediately went to her. She slid down the wall, breaking into uncontrollable sobs. I held her and tried to comfort her the best I could.

Two weeks later we moved into a government housing project. To make money to take care of us, Mama sewed. She was the best seamstress around and could make anything. Still, there never seemed to be enough money, but we got by somehow. My step-father offered Mama money, but her pride would not let her take it.

How can he do this to her? *I had quietly wondered.* How can he do this to us?

I shake my head. *Then it happened to me. I should*

have known it would. It's only fair.

Pulling my thoughts back to the present, I glance over at Chance, meeting his concerned expression.

"Sorry, when it comes to my past, I have a habit of zoning out every now and then."

"Thanks for letting me know," he says with a smile.

"No problem."

❅❅❅

My mouth drops open in awe when we finally pull into Chance's driveway. His home is a renovated Victorian, built a little over a hundred years ago. It reminds me of the wooden doll house I had as a child. The red brick structure is massive, the forest green trim the perfect compliment to the stylish house. White laced curtains cover the windows and the landscaping in and around the circular driveway is immaculate. Mama and I used to dream about us one day living in a place like this.

Chance gets out and opens my door, then grabs my shopping bags from the back seat. On the way over, we stopped by the mall and he took me shopping. When I protested, he told me to consider it an advance against my salary. I had agreed, but somehow I know he's going to come up with an excuse not to take my money. If I've learned anything this morning, it is the type of man he is–giving, caring, and very strong-willed. And I can't begin to express how much I am looking forward to a shower and clean clothes. It's been a while since I've had either.

"Thank you," I tell him as he hands me a few of the bags.

"You're very welcome."

Chance shows me around the place, then takes me up to my room, which happens to be right next to his. This is both unsettling and comforting. But as I take in the amazing mix of Victorian and contemporary decor, I have to smile. With its lace bedding, hardwood floor and white leather sofa and chair, the room is absolutely perfect.

"It's beautiful," I tell him.

"I'm glad you like it. Of all the rooms in the house, this one seemed more like you. And don't ask me how I knew."

"I'm glad you were so inspired."

He smiles. "So am I."

We stand for a moment, silently staring at one another, neither of us knowing what else to say. He finally moves toward the door.

"I'll leave you to get settled. I thought I might order a pizza for dinner. Is that okay with you?"

I wordlessly nod. After not having it for so long, pizza sounds heavenly. "Chance." He stops, turning back to me. "Thank you . . . for everything."

"You're welcome, Cosset. I would do anything for you."

He leaves before I can respond. But the new inner warmth his parting words invoke remains.

❋❋❋

Why now, God?

For a week now, have lain in this warm comfortable bed with my stomach fuller than it has been in a long time. I have a job and I am blessed to live in this beautiful home. I have every reason to be happy, yet the sad memories of the past plague me and I can't get to sleep, no matter how hard I try. I can't understand it. Why is this new, longed-for sense of security dredging everything up now? Why are the pains of the past becoming so prominent?

First come the memories of losing my brother.

Sitting in the emergency room lobby waiting to hear about Nate, I struggled to get a mental handle on what happened. I had been at work when I got the call. A drunk driver hit my brother. I was on the verge of possibly losing the last important person in my life. Nate had his whole life ahead of him. He was handsome, funny, smart, and made the world a better place by just being here. He was the bright light in my life and had the potential to do great things. If I lost him, I didn't know what to do. I didn't think I could handle it.

"Dr. Callahan, how is my brother?" I was past the tears by then and I knew it was time to be brave.

"Miss Allen, your brother is in critical condition," the doctor answered. "His neck is broken, his right leg is broken in two places, and he has a punctured lung. He has a very serious concussion and is still unconscious, but we've managed to stabilize him for now. It was a very hard hit he

took and he has a long way to go before he is out of the woods. He's in intensive care and will be constantly monitored for any changes."

My legs weakening, I grabbed the back of the chair for support. "Can I see him?"

"Yes, you can. And I knew you would probably want to stay with him tonight, so I took the liberty of sending for a cot and a blanket."

It was as if he could read my mind. Nate was all I had left in the world and I had no intention of leaving.

Dr. Callahan took me in to see Nate. As soon as I walked into the room, the tears began again. He looked so weak and helpless, things I could never recall my brother being before. Watching the machine breathe for him literally broke my heart.

Reaching his bedside, I sat in the chair and lightly rested my head against Nate's chest, listening to his shallow breathing, praying he would live through this.

Dr. Callahan came back a while later to check him again and informed me there was no change. Instead of setting up the cot, I grabbed the blanket and rested my head against Nate's side, falling asleep with a prayer on my lips.

Two hours later, Nate's heart stopped and he passed

away.

Then come the memories of losing Mama.

I rested my head against one side of Mama's hospital bed with Nate on the other. She was no longer coherent, but I prayed she knew we were there. She was past the pain, and though I longed for her suffering to end, it was still hard to let her go, and even harder for my brother.

"Don't leave us, Mama," Nate tearfully pleaded.

Unable to pull my gaze from Mama's beautiful calm face, I was so emotional, my brain couldn't form words. We were losing our mother, and nothing could change that. I had never experienced anything so painful in my life.

"I love you, Mama," I finally whispered. "I love you so much."

An hour later, she went to sleep and never awakened.

Then my thoughts shift to my stepfather's abandonment. Though it was years ago, part of me has never been able to get over Dave's betrayal. He was my father, and I couldn't have loved him more if we shared the same blood. I remember thinking I would marry someone just like him one day. At the time I had no idea how true that prediction would be. But I didn't marry someone just like him, I married someone twice as bad, and I lost my little girl in the process.

A soft sob escapes me as long-buried grief breaks through to the surface. Oh, how I miss my Heather. Rocking back and forth, the sobs racking my body change to wails and my emotions explode, the pain in my heart excruciating. Everything I'd blocked out while living on the streets comes out in a rush.

A moment later, my head is buried against a warm chest and I am encircled in a pair of strong arms.

"Shhh, it's okay. I'm here."

"It . . . it hurts . . . Oh, it hurts . . . so much!"

"I know, baby," he croons. "I know. It's going to be okay."

"I miss my little girl," I cry, clutching the back of his t-shirt. "I was her mother and I couldn't even protect her."

"Shhh, don't. You were a good mother and there was nothing you could have done. It wasn't your fault."

My brain tries to accept his words, but my heart fights against it. Add to this the aching loneliness that fills me, the pain is excruciating. I continue to cling to him, soaking in his warmth.

Lying down next to me, Chance puts his feet up,

holding me close, and I burrow deeper in his embrace as a new round of sobs escape.

"Shhh, it's all right," he continues to softly croon, burying his face in my hair.

"Stay and hold me, okay?"

He pulls the comforter over us both Pressing a kiss to my forehead, he whispers, "I'm here, honey. And I'm not going anywhere."

Chance's arms are a safe haven, and in them I find comfort. If only for a while.

***

A month later

Chance smiles at me from across the table as we finish our breakfast. Working for him has been wonderful, and it feels less like work and more like enjoying . . . well, just *being*. Since I've been here, I have slowly been able to discover me again, only it goes a lot deeper. I never thought I could ever feel this way. It is all so new to me. I mean, sure I have been married, but

Jake had thrown my trust away long before he died. Ours had not been a marriage of real love, but of necessity. And with me being three months pregnant, we had decided it was best. Looking back, I can see how wrong we were. And had I remained single and raised my child alone, maybe she would still be . . .

No, not today.

Chance's warm hand covers mine. I look up and try to will the sadness and guilt from my features, but it is becoming increasingly evident that I can't hide anything from him.

"Is it time for another pep talk?"

"No," I sigh dramatically, then smile. "I think I'm good."

He smiles back. "I know you are. And because you are doing so well, I would like to take you out tonight."

Swallowing hard, my smile fades slightly. "You mean, like a date?"

"Yes, I mean a date."

"I don't know . . ." Despite my strong feelings for him–feelings that continue to grow with each passing second–I am afraid. I'm afraid to letting him into my heart only to be abandoned later. I couldn't handle losing yet another person. "Maybe that isn't such a good idea right now."

"Cosset, look at me." I bravely raise my eyes to his ruggedly handsome face. "I love you, Cosset, and I know you have feelings for me."

"I'm sorry," I whisper, getting up. "I can't." Feeling the coming of unwanted tears, I turn to leave, but his hand catches mine before I even make it to the doorway.

Moving behind me, he wraps his arms around my waist, pressing me back against his muscular chest. My eyes slip shut as my body melts against his. Truthfully, I *am* in love with him, pure and simple. I couldn't deny it even if I tried.

But I am still afraid.

Over the past month, Chance has made his feelings crystal clear. He has comforted me when I have needed comfort, been a listening ear, and an amazing friend. Though he has never pushed himself on me and has showered me with all the affection I have longed for but never had until him, I can't seem to let go of the fear and hurt I've carried inside for so long.

And more than anything, I don't think I am good

enough for him. I feel unworthy, like I don't deserve someone like him. I'll never belong in his world. I guess I have lived on the streets too long to see it any other way.

"Don't," he whispers against my ear, his warm breath melting my insides like butter in a hot skillet. "You are worth more than you can possibly know." He kisses my ear and a heady sigh escapes me. What this man does to me with a simple touch! "You are an amazing woman, and I need you to know, I'm so in love with you, I can't think straight half the time."

"You can't . . ." I try to pull away, but he holds me fast against his solid warm body.

"I know you don't believe I can truly love you, but you are wrong. Let me prove it to you, Cosset. Let me show you how much you mean to me. Give me a chance to prove to you that having your love is worth everything, that owning your heart would be a priceless gift."

I turn in his arms just as tears begin to spill down my cheeks. His words are beautiful, and I desperately want to believe him, because I lost my heart to him the moment I awakened in his car and glimpsed his face.

And it hadn't been because of his looks, but because of the raw emotion I saw in his eyes when he met my gaze, the sincerity that had been written in his expression.

You are so good. Too good for me.

"Trust me," he whispers, touching his forehead to mine. "Trust me to prove my love to you. Trust me with your heart." The warmth of his breath fans my lips and they part. Then he presses his glorious mouth to mine and my knees go weak, which only serves to have him hold me even closer, every inch of me longing to be a part of him. His mouth is warm and sweet, like the melon he'd eaten a moment ago. His tongue sensuously moves against mine and I lose all sense of time and place. I allow my hands to explore his masculine waist and travel of his sculpted back, over his chiseled biceps, and finally bury my fingers in his soft, thick hair. He moans, deepening the kiss even more and I am on fire. His own hands travel everywhere, searing a burning path, branding me in each place he touches.

I love him. I don't know how this can be happening to me, but I love him with every fiber of my being.

Slowly parting his mouth from mine, his kiss moves to my neck, then to my exposed shoulder, making me grateful for whoever invented tank tops. I'm sure it was a guy.

Chance is ever a gentleman during his passionate ministrations, which makes me love him all the more. The feel of his tongue against my skin causes a combination of heat and chills to come over me and goosebumps erupt on my arms. No one has ever made me feel so much at once. When his mouth finally returns to mine, I sigh.

"Promise you won't break my heart," I murmur. "Promise me."

He draws back a little to look into my eyes, emotion stirring in his gaze. "I promise you, baby. I won't break your heart. I never will."

Swallowing hard, I finally say, "I love you, Chance. And I'll trust you with my heart."

❀❀❀

Chance
Chance's insides completely melt with her words.

He has been in agony for the past month, desperately longing to hear her speak them, and to have them be true. And there is no doubt in his mind of Cosset's sincerity. He knows her well enough to know she would never lie to him. She doesn't have a pretentious bone in her body. Trusting in someone again enough to give her whole heart is new to her. In fact, everything about this is completely out of her comfort zone and he empathizes.

But Chance knows there is nothing Cosset can't overcome. This is a new life for them both, and he is determined to love her through it and whatever comes, both the good and the bad. She is meant to be his. For the longest time, he wondered if he would ever be able to truly love a woman, to give himself completely. His question had been answered the moment he caught a glimpse of Cosset sitting on the shelter bench, her long, dark curls cascading from under a red baseball cap, and the sun adding a shimmer to her light brown skin. It was as if everything in his life suddenly made sense, like he finally had a purpose for existing. Sure, some would call him crazy, but Chance knows different. His mind has never been so clear.

Pressing his lips to her ear, he whispers, "I have something to ask you and I don't want to frighten you away." He draws back a little, meeting her gaze. "Will you marry me, Cosset? Will you take my name and share my life? I promise I will do everything in my power to never hurt you. Will you be my wife and trust in that?"

He watches the growing smile spread across her beautiful face, her eyes filling with tears. Her warm hand caresses his face and she give him her answer.

"Yes."

His mouth meets hers again and his world shifts as everything in his life falls into place.

❀❀❀

The following morning, we go shopping for rings, a white dress and other things we will need for a quick intimate wedding. We plan to exchange our vows next week beneath the white gazebo in the back yard. Other than the preacher and his wife, it will be just be the two of us. I've frequently pondered how sad it is that neither of us have family to invite, then I remind myself that Chance is my family now, and I am his. Nothing else matters.

✻✻✻

We stop by a diner to grab a quick lunch. Sitting across from each other in a cozy booth, Chance takes my hands in his, gifting me with the heart-palpitating smile I have come to know so well. There are moments that I still wonder how I've garnered his love and what I have done to warrant such a blessing. But I continually remind myself not to question, and to just accept and be grateful. No amount of gratitude will ever be enough. From now until forever, I will be thanking God for this amazing man, and for his unconditional love.

He gently squeezes my hands. "I love you."

"And I love you." The words that should seem foreign to me are spoken to one another with ease. Our mutual smiles are loving. His full mouth curves up, hypnotizing me, making me long to be alone with him and resume the passionate affection that has unwaveringly generated so much heat between us since yesterday.

"I think you are reading my mind," I say and he nods.

"Oh, yeah."

A sexy arch of his brow has me suddenly using my menu as a fan. "Where is our server?" I mumble and he laughs.

"Patience, my love. Patience."

"I can do patience," I reply, giving him a siren look of my own. He quickly picks up his menu and I laugh, then I open mine and try to decide what I would like.

Hearing the ding of the bell on the door, I glance up and freeze, unable to believe what I am seeing. Entering the bar is the last person I ever expected to see again.

"Dave."

✻✻✻

His name comes out as a hoarse whisper.

"What?" Chance quickly turns as my stepfather's eyes meet mine, and Dave seems to be just as shocked to see me as I am to see him. He actually recognizes me. After all these years, he still recognizes me. He slowly approaches our table.

"Hello, Cosset."

"Hello." I say back, managing to keep my voice monotone despite the anxiety and anger hovering near the surface.

"How have you been?" he asks.

How do you think? I hesitate before answering. "I have been good," I lie. "And you?" It takes every ounce of strength I have to remain cordial.

He doesn't answer. "You are looking well."

His nonchalance completely annoys me. "How is your wife? Better than you treated your first one, I hope." My voice is colder than I intended. Or maybe I did. I am sad, angry and hurt.

You abandoned us. You abandoned Mama. And me. No excuse he uses could ever be good enough. Seeing my stepfather is more painful than I ever thought it would be. Never in my wildest dreams had I imagined seeing him again.

Dave's smile seems sad. "Sweet, beautiful Cosset. You were always the protector." His expression grows serious. "I never got married." He pauses. "My parents have disowned me then and there because of it, but it was a decision I had to make." When I say nothing, he sighs. "I've really missed you, Cosset. I've missed being your father."

"So, you think you can just waltz back into my life just like that? Well, I've been without a father this long, I'm pretty sure I'll be okay."

"But I won't." Surprisingly, tears fill his eyes.

Silence surrounds us for a moment until Chance's voice slices through it. He introduces himself as my fiancee. Putting his arm around me, he kisses my temple and whispers, "You two need to talk." He gets up and offers Dave his spot, then walks over to the jukebox.

Dave sits down and it is a full minute before he speaks again. I sense his hesitance as he slowly fills me in on everything he has been doing all these years. He expresses his sorrow over Mama's death. He says he wanted to attend the funeral, but he had been too ashamed to show up, so he grieved for her privately.

My icy heart melting slightly, I begrudgingly tell him about Nate and tears again fill his eyes. He had no idea Nate passed away and the grief is clearly written in his expression.

"I never expected to see you again," he says.

I lower my eyes. "I didn't ever expect to see you again either." *And I never wanted to . . . until now.* Despite my best efforts, my thoughts and emotions are betraying me.

Dave heaves a deep sigh and it is another full minute before he speaks again. "I still care for you, Cosset–very much. And I wish I could take back all the hurt I caused you and your mother, and Nate." He pauses a moment, rubbing a hand over his face. "I couldn't marry the other woman. My family wanted me to be in love with her, and I thought maybe I could force myself to be."

I really don't want to hear this and I start to interrupt, but he continues.

"I'm not blaming my choices on anyone else. I made them all on my own and I've accepted the blame for what happened. I let the pressure get to me. I let what was important slip away. For that, I am so sorry. More sorry than I can possibly express. I know words aren't good enough, and if it takes me the rest of my life to prove that I have changed, then so be it."

Silently staring out the diner window, I ponder his

words. I glance across the dining room at Chance, meeting his concerned stare. I smile slightly, trying to assure him I'm okay. His mouthed *I love you* gives me comfort.

I finally return my eyes to Dave. It has been eighteen years since he walked out on us. The day he told Mama about the other woman was the last time I saw him. Still, I remember everything about him, every single detail of his face.

Time hasn't changed him much. He is still very handsome. His sandy-blond hair looks freshly cut, only now he wears it shorter on the sides and back. But his blue eyes don't hold the same sparkle they once did. Now that I am really looking at him, he looks tired. I have really missed him. And I can't deny it any longer.

"What is it you want from me?" I finally find the strength to ask.

"I don't mean to cause you pain, Cosset. That is the last thing I want to do. I'm so ashamed of what I did. I know I can't expect anything from you and . . . I have no right to ask, but . . ."

I can tell this is hard for him, and not because of pride. I honestly think he fears what I will say. It is that vulnerability that melts the last of the ice in my heart.

"I hope one day you can forgive me," he continues. "I know I am asking a lot and you don't have to say anything. I just ask for your forgiveness. And I won't try to push you."

Again I look away, furiously blinking back the stinging tears that come unbidden and unwelcome.

He stands to leave. "No matter what, I'm glad I had the chance to see you, Cosset. You mean more to me than you could possibly know."

I heave a deep sigh, part of me unable to believe this is really happening. Before I can talk myself out of it, I reach into my purse and take out a piece of paper and a pen. I write down my address and phone number and hold it out to him. "If you ever want to call, or come by . . ." I don't finish.

Dave takes the paper, closing his hand over mine, tears filling his eyes.

"Thank you. I will call if that's okay."

I'm still wary, but I nod.

Goodbye, Dad. As I watch him walk away, feelings I thought were long since buried and gone quickly stirring in my heart once more. But self-preservation is still very much ingrained in me, and I can't let him get too close. Too much has happened.

God, I don't know if I can do this. Please help me.

***

At Chance's gentle urging, I allow my heart to open to my father. And yes, I have started thinking of him that way because he is the only father I have ever known, and I still love him, despite the past.

Two days later, Dave comes by to see me and we begin to connect and get to know each other. I share my life's experiences with him, telling him about my previous marriage, the loss of my child and my home, and my year-long experience living on the streets. It is hard to share these things because I don't not want his pity. Tears are shed tears as we talk about all we have lost. But we have both grown much. This past week I have learned to not close myself off, and through the years, Dave has learned how to live his own life and not let others live it for him.

Though my feelings for my father have grown, and

continue to grow each time I see him, I am still afraid. I don't think I could bear to be hurt that way again, so I remain cautious. Each time I feel him getting too close, I pull back. I can't make it easy for him.

✳✳✳

Two days before the wedding, Dave stops by. After saying hello and talking with Chance a moment, Chance kisses me and makes himself scarce to give us some privacy.

"I have something for you," Dave says, handing me a wrapped box.

"Thank you." I am surprised. I hadn't expected anything from him. I haven't even invited him to our wedding. Having him stand by my side is something I long for, but my emotions are still jumbled.

He sits next to me on the sofa and watches me open the gift. I smile as I gazed down at the white and powder blue-striped photo album. The words *My Family* are on the cover in raised lettering, accented by colorful silk daisies. As I open the album, I gasp, hot tears immediately spilling down my cheeks as gaze at the family photo of Mama, Dave, me and Nate. I had been eight and Nate four when we had the picture taken at the mall in front of a large Christmas tree. I flip through the pages, crying more with each photograph.

I finally raise my eyes in disbelief. "When did you do this? And how did you find all of these pictures?"

"I found the photos packed in a box in the attic last year. I put the album together yesterday." He flipped through to the blank pages. "You are about to have a family of your own, and even if we can never be close, I just wanted you to have this for your children."

Smiling, I reach for his hand. He is so different. He really has changed, and it thrills me to finally be able to see it.

"I forgive you, Dad." I squeeze his hand tighter. "For everything. And I am sure Mama does, too."

It is obvious my words have caught him by surprise, especially, I am sure, hearing me call him Dad. For a moment he doesn't say anything. I watch various emotions play across his face, tears quickly pooling in his eyes.

"Thank you," he finally says, his voice soft.

His tone humbles me and my heart is full of love. I

place the album on the table. "Dad, please forgive me for being so cold to you. Forgive me for . . ."

He pulls me into his warm embrace and words leave me. Holding onto him, I cry against his shoulder, shedding the sorrows I have held onto for years.

"There is nothing to forgive," he says, weeping openly. "You weren't cold to me. You were still hurting, and you had reason to be. But I will make you a promise. I promise you I will never, ever do anything to hurt you again."

Kissing his cheek, I ask, "Will you stand beside me at my wedding?"

"Nothing would make me happier."

Hearing a sniffle, I look toward the doorway and find Chance wiping his eyes, his smile slowly widening. I reach out and he joins us.

Sitting between the two men I love more than anything in the world, I send up a prayer of gratitude for yet another precious gift. A month ago I had nothing, and now I have everything I have longed for and more.

It is indeed a new life for me. One that I will embrace with everything in me, and never again take for granted.

✻✻✻

Six months later

Lying in bed beneath the large skylight, completely spent from making love all evening, Chance holds me close as we gaze up at the star-filled sky. Every moment spent in his arms is heavenly, and there is no other place I would rather be. I smile as his lips brush my ear.

"I love you," he tells me.

"I know, and I love you."

I feel him smile against my cheek and his fingers toy with my wedding rings. "You never did tell me your news."

"Well, how could I? You've kept me busy all evening."

"So, are you saying when we make love, you can't think of anything else?"

I snort. "I can't *think* at all."

"And this is my fault how?"

I laugh, nudging him. "You know how. Whenever

you start kissing me, it totally obliterates my self-control and makes my mind go blank."

"And I am extremely proud to possess that talent. Especially since you do the same thing to me."

"I'm proud of it as well."

"He kisses me again. "So, the news?"

Smiling, I press a hand against his face, caressing the soft, groomed stubble, happiness filling my insides. "Our family is about to grow by one."

Chance draws back and turns on the lamp, the sheen of tears in his eyes matching my own. "You're pregnant? Really?"

"Really."

"Okay, you have *got* to let me be the one to tell Dave he is going to be a grandpa. The guy is still too good-looking and youthful for his age. Calling him grandpa will give him a few more gray hairs."

I laugh. "I would never deprive you of that joy. Besides, it will definitely make Beth feel better." I smile as I think of the woman Dad has been dating for the past month. The two met when she applied for a secretary position at his construction business. She and Dad are the same age, but she is always saying Dad was blessed with better genes because the gray at his temples only serves to make him more handsome. A full-blooded Cherokee Indian, Beth's exotic features are beautiful, and Dad frequently makes sure she knows. And Chance does the same for me, telling and showing me each day. He treats me like a queen, making me feel loved and treasured. To have someone actually put me first is the most amazing thing. Simply put, we are everything to one another. And it will always be this way.

Snuggling closer, I softly caress my husband's lips. "Thank you," I say, my voice a little hoarse with emotion, pressing his hand against my stomach. "Thank you for this gift. For giving me a part of you, and for giving me the privilege of being a mother again."

His arms tighten around me. "Thank *you*," he murmurs against my mouth. "For giving me my life back."

About J. Adams

J. (Jewel) Adams stays crazy busy with her family and writing. She has written several books in different genres, mainly romance, and is also a motivational speaker to both youth and adult audiences.
She is on the last leg of home schooling her two youngest, and between that and conjuring up new ideas for her books, her brain is completely fried most of the time. She and her husband Sean are the parents of eight children and grandparents to five, which means they are both losing hair, but hey, that's what Rogaine is for, right?
In her spare time (when she has any) she likes to curl up with a good book and a healthy stash of orange Tic Tacs. She and her family reside in Utah.
Jewel loves hearing from her fans, so if you would like to contact her to tell her how much you love her books or give her sympathy for the fried brain, or suggestions

for the hair loss problem (for her
husband, of course) contact her at jewela40@gmail.com
To check out Jewel's other books, visit her website at
JewelAdams.com
And stop by her blog: **jewelsbestgems.blogspot.com**

Other books by J. Adams/Jewel Adams
Still His Woman
The Legacy
The Wishing Hour
Tears of Heaven
Place In This World
The Journey
Against the Odds
Mercedes' Mountain
Guardian of My Heart
Sweet 21 Birthday Ball

Ebooks
The Wishing Hour
The Legacy
Tears of Heaven
Place In This World: The Sequel to The Journey
The Journey
Mercedes' Mountain
That Kind of Love
The Shelter of His Arms
What the Heart Sees
The Sound of Love
Stories of the Heart
Against the Odds
Guardian of My Heart
Elise's Heart

J. Adams

For Love of Angel
Sweet 21 Birthday Ball
Say What You Need to Say

Children's Book
Forbidden Portals: The Quicksilver Project